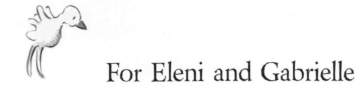

For Eleni and Gabrielle

First published in the UK in 2020
by New Frontier Publishing Europe Ltd
Uncommon, 126 New King's Road, London, SW6 4LZ
www.newfrontierpublishing.co.uk

ISBN: 978-1-912858-39-2

A CIP catalogue record for this book is available from the British Library.

Designed by Celeste Hulme

Printed and bound in China
1 3 5 7 9 10 8 6 4 2

THE BOY ON THE PAGE

Peter Carnavas

One quiet morning, a small boy landed on the page.

At first, there was nothing else.

Then very slowly, a world began to appear.

New life emerged. Things started to grow ...
and so did the boy.

But as he wandered through his new world,

one question troubled him.

Why was he here?

The boy looked around the page and then before he knew it

he was doing all sorts of things.
He rolled down a hill.

He rode a horse.

He caught a shiny, silver fish.

He planted a tree.

He paddled a canoe.

He played an accordion.

He saved a small animal.

He stood in the pouring rain.

He painted a portrait.

The boy grew up ...

and he fell in love.

He climbed a mountain.

He saw the whole world in somebody's eyes.

He built a house.

He gave someone lunch ...

and a place to stay.

He grew vegetables.

He trained a dog.

He put out a fire.

But every now and then, as the moon rolled through the deep, blue sky, he still wondered why he had landed on the page.

Looking for answers, he tried something he
had never tried before.

He jumped off the page ...

only to tumble straight back.

And waiting for him there
was everything he had ever made,
every animal he had ever cared for
and every person he had ever loved.

At last, he knew.
He knew why he was here.